This Little Tiger book belongs to:

_____

_____

_____

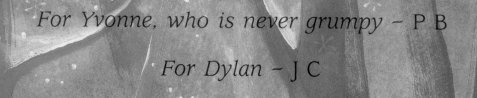

For Yvonne, who is never grumpy – P B

For Dylan – J C

LITTLE TIGER PRESS LTD,
an imprint of the Little Tiger Group
1 Coda Studios, 189 Munster Road, London SW6 6AW
www.littletiger.co.uk
First published in Great Britain 2009
This edition published 2014
Text copyright © Paul Bright 2009 • Illustrations copyright © Jane Chapman 2009
Visit Jane Chapman at www.ChapmanandWarnes.com
Paul Bright and Jane Chapman have asserted their rights to be identified as the
author and illustrator of this work under the Copyright, Designs and Patents Act, 1988
A CIP catalogue record for this book is available from the British Library
All rights reserved • ISBN 978-1-84869-078-3
Printed in China • LTP/1800/2843/0719
4 6 8 10 9 7 5

Grumpy Badger's Christmas

Paul Bright   Jane Chapman

LITTLE TIGER

LONDON

It was almost Christmas, and the forest was a flurry of activity. The animals were bustling here and there – putting up the Christmas tree, wrapping presents, making tasty puddings and pies – while the young ones scampered about, squeaking with excitement.

Everybody was looking
forward to Christmas.
Well, *almost* everybody . . . .

Grumpy Badger looked out of his window
and scowled.

"Happy Christmas!" shouted Squirrel.

"Happy Christmas? Bah!" he shouted back.
"What piffle! I am a sensible creature
and I sleep all through the cold winter.

"Now I am going to bed until the spring, and if anyone wakes me I shall be very, very grumpy!" And with that, he pulled his window shut with a

CLUNK!

Grumpy Badger knew he would be hungry
when he woke, so he checked his larder.
There were puddings, pickles and pastries,
packets of hams and cheeses, crispy crackers,
jars of fruit and sticky-sweet jams.
"That *should* do," he said.

Then he filled his hot water bottle
and climbed into bed.
He had just closed his eyes when
there was a knock at the door.

KNOCK!

KNOCK!

KNOCK!

It was Mole.

"H-h-happy Christmas, Mr Badger," he said,
timidly. "I'm sorry to bother you. I've been trying
to put lights on the Christmas tree, but it's just
too big. Could I please borrow your ladder?"

"Christmas tree?" spluttered Grumpy Badger. "Piffle and double piffle! Christmas is for sleeping – and that's what I'm trying to do!" And he closed the door with a

BANG!

"Bah!" huffed Grumpy Badger, climbing into bed. "Borrow my ladder indeed! All I want is a bit of peace and quiet and leave-me-alone."

He peeked under his bed, where he'd put more food for springtime: candies and cookies and cherry cup-cakes.

Then he cuddled deep into his big, warm eiderdown. He was just starting to snore when there was another knock at the door.

KNOCK!
KNOCK!
KNOCK!

This time it was Squirrel. "Hello, Badger," he said, cheerily. "I've brought you a Christmas present."

"Christmas present?" snorted Grumpy Badger.

"Piffle and triple piffle!
I don't like presents and I don't like Christmas!
All I want is a little peace!" And he shut the
door with a CRASH!

Now Grumpy Badger was really grumpy. To cheer himself up, he thought about the bottles and bottles of home-made lemonade he had in the cellar. Then he lay down and closed his eyes. But he couldn't sleep – his head felt a little chilly. Suddenly there was a loud banging at the door.

BANG!
BANG!
BANG!

"Oh, what is it *now*?" Grumpy Badger sighed. He was about as tired and grumpy as a Badger can be.

"Oh, Badger," panted Rabbit. "Help! It's poor Mole. He's stuck at the top of the Christmas tree. Come quickly!"

"PIFFLE!" shouted Grumpy Badger.
"And triple piffle with knobs on!
Why can't everyone just leave me alone?" And he slammed
the door so hard that the whole house shook!

SLAM!

At long last, Grumpy Badger fell asleep.
But soon he was tossing and turning
and wriggling and squirming. He was
dreaming of Mole, dangling by one
tiny paw from the top of an enormous
Christmas tree. Mole was trembling.
Mole was losing his grip.

Mole was about to fall!

"NOOOOOO!"
screamed Grumpy Badger,
sitting bolt upright, and
suddenly wide awake.

"What have I done?"

he yelled. He jumped out of bed, grabbed
his ladder and dashed into the street.

Grumpy Badger raced up to
the Christmas tree.

"Hold on, Mole!" he cried.

He scrambled up the
ladder, scooped Mole
gently into his arms,
then helped him
down to the ground.

"I'm so sorry," said Grumpy Badger.

"What a grumpy old fool I've been."

"You're a hero now!" said Squirrel, and he gave
Badger back his Christmas present – a soft,
fluffy nightcap.

"But I've been so grouchy," said Grumpy Badger.
"What can I do to make things better?"

And then he knew.

Badger's Christmas party was the best ever. There were puddings, pickles and pastries, cheeses and hams and sticky-sweet jams, cookies and cup-cakes and bottles and bottles of home-made lemonade.

They jigged and jived and joked and laughed, late into the night.

"Happy Christmas, everybody!"
Badger cried. "And if you don't all
come to my party next year,

I SHALL BE
VERY
GRUMPY
INDEED!"